Moose, Goose, Animals on the Loose!

Geraldo Valério

A CANADIAN WILDLIFE ABC

Owlkids Books

Here they come ...
Canadian animals running, jumping,
swimming, and roaring your way!

Aa

Now arriving...
Arctic Fox

Beaver
building
branch by branch

Bb

big
bold
Bison

Cc

Caribou
caring
cuddling

Calf

Dd

Dragonflies

dart

and

dip

Eagle

Ee

Eat,
eaglet!
Eat!

Eaglet

Ff

Frog
feasting on flies

Gg

Canada
Goose

Gosling   grazing
on grass

Hh

Hare

Hop!
Hop!
Hop!

Ii

Ivory Gulls
in flight

Jj

jiggle

joggle

Jellyfish

Kk

king-sized
Killer Whale

Ll

Loons
laughing
on the lake

Mm

magnificent
mighty
Moose

Nn

Narwhal
native of the
North

Otter

out on the ocean

Pp

powerful
playful
Polar Bear

Qq

quiet
Quail

Rr

ring-tailed
Raccoon

Ss

striped
Skunk

T is for trio:

Turtle

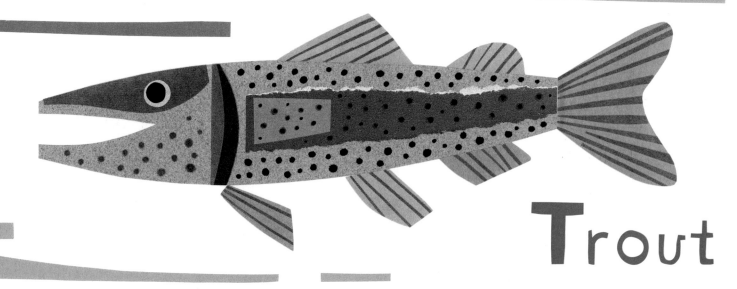

Tt

Toad

Trout

BelUga
upside down

WalrUs
under water

Uu

Vv

voracious
Vultures

WOOO ... WOOO ...

Ww

Wolf!

exuberant
MuskoX

exotic Lyn**X**

Xx

Yellowthroat

Yellow Jacket

Yy

Yellowlegs

Yellow!

Yellow!

Yellow!

fuzzy
grizzly
GriZZly
Bears

Aa
Arctic Fox
The Arctic fox's deep, thick fur and bushy wraparound tail help to keep it warm in winter.

Bb
Beaver
The beaver uses its big, strong front teeth to cut down trees for food and for building dams and lodges.

Bison
In winter, the bison uses its large head to push away snow, so it can eat the grasses underneath.

Cc
Caribou
Every year, caribou shed their antlers and then grow a new, larger pair.

Dd
Dragonfly

Two pairs of strong wings allow the dragonfly to fly in any direction and to travel long distances.

Ee
Eagle
The bald eagle builds its nest out of branches. It is one of the largest bird's nests in the world, and can be as big as a large hot tub.

Ff
Frog

The frog uses its quick, sticky tongue to catch flies and other insects.

Gg
Canada Goose
When they are only two days old, Canada goose goslings are able to walk, swim, and find their own food. They eat plants, grain, berries, and grasses.

Hh

Hare
The snowshoe hare has large hind feet that, like snowshoes, keep it from sinking into the snow.

Ii

Ivory Gull
The ivory gull lives year-round in the Far North, close to the pack ice.

Jj
Jellyfish
Jellyfish, or jellies, have stinging tentacles that are used to stun and capture their prey.

Kk
Killer Whale
The killer or orca whale is the largest member of the dolphin family. A full-grown male can be as long as a big yellow school bus.

Ll

Loon
The loon is pictured on the reverse side of the Canadian one-dollar coin, giving the coin its popular name: the loonie.

Mm

Moose
Moose are powerful swimmers. They wade into rivers and lakes to browse on water plants and to cool down.

Nn
Narwhal
The male narwhal's long ivory tusk is really a tooth, which continues to grow throughout the animal's life.

Oo

Otter
The sea otter has a flap of skin under each front leg where it stores food, as well as a rock, which it uses as a tool to break open shellfish.

Pp
Polar Bear
The thick black pads on a polar bear's feet have small, soft bumps that give the bear good grip and make it sure-footed on ice.

Qq
Quail

The northern bobwhite's dappled reddish-brown and white feathers are good camouflage and make the bird hard to spot.

Rr
Raccoon
A raccoon is able to climb headfirst down a tree by turning its hind feet so that they point backwards.

Ss
Skunk

Skunks release a smelly spray when threatened. Luckily, their markings make them easy to recognize — and avoid.

Tt
Toad

Toads hibernate for the winter. Some burrow in the ground. Others stay deep in logs or under leaf litter.

Trout

Like all fish, rainbow trout breathe through gills.

Turtle
The turtle's flat shell and webbed feet help it to swim and dive.

Uu
Beluga
Beluga whales have a thick layer of fat, or blubber, that helps to keep them warm in cold Arctic water.

Walrus
Walruses use their long tusks to pull their huge bodies out of the water and to make breathing holes in the ice.

Vv
Vulture
The turkey vulture is a large bird that uses its sense of smell to find its food: dead animals.

Ww
Wolf

Wolves howl to call their pack together, to sound an alarm, and to communicate over long distances.

Xx
Lynx
The bobcat, a type of lynx, is about two times larger than a domestic cat, and is a fierce hunter.

Muskox
When threatened, a muskox herd forms a circle with calves in the middle and adults on the outside, with their big heads and horns facing outward.

Yy
Yellowlegs
The greater yellowlegs feeds in shallow water. It sweeps the tip of its long bill from side to side to scoop up food.

Yellowthroat
The common yellowthroat is a small songbird with a loud, fast *witchety-witchety-witchety* song.

Yellow Jacket
A single queen starts a yellow jacket nest in the spring. By fall, the nest can be the size of a basketball.

Zz
Grizzly Bear
Mother grizzly bears are very protective of their young and will attack if they think their cubs are in danger.

Owlkids Books acknowledges the financial support of the
Canada Council for the Arts, the Ontario Arts Council,
the Government of Canada through the Canada Book
Fund (CBF) and the Government of Ontario through the
Ontario Media Development Corporation's Book Initiative
for our publishing activities.

Published in Canada by
Owlkids Books Inc.
10 Lower Spadina Avenue
Toronto, ON M5V 2Z2

Published in the United States by
Owlkids Books Inc.
1700 Fourth Street
Berkeley, CA 94710

Library and Archives Canada Cataloguing in Publication

Valerio, Geraldo, author illustrator
    Moose, goose, animals on the loose! : a Canadian wildlife ABC / Geraldo Valério.

ISBN 978-1-77147-174-9 (hardback)

    1. English language--Alphabet--Juvenile literature. 2. Animals--Canada--
Pictorial works--Juvenile literature. 3. Alphabet books. I. Title.

PE1155.V34 2016   j421'.1   C2015-907944-6

Library of Congress Control Number: 2015957722

The artwork in this book was rendered in paper collage.
Edited by Debbie Rogosin
Designed by Claudia Dávila

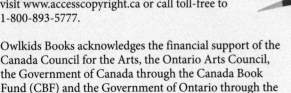

 ONTARIO ARTS COUNCIL
CONSEIL DES ARTS DE L'ONTARIO
an Ontario government agency
un organisme du gouvernement de l'Ontario

Canada Council   Conseil des Arts
for the Arts   du Canada

Canadä

Manufactured in Shenzhen, Guangdong, China, in April 2017, by WKT Co. Ltd.
Job #16CB4027

B   C   D   E   F

OWL kids   Publisher of Chirp, chickaDEE and OWL | Owlkids Books is a division of    Bayard CANADA
www.owlkidsbooks.com